A POLICE OFFICER...
that's what I'll be!

Written by Police Officer Ronald Pinkston
Illustrated by Israel Rivera

QUEBECOR
Printing/Kingsport

ISBN 0-9671708-0-X $12.99

51299

9 780967 170800

Israel Rivera used watercolors and ink
to create the illustrations for the inside of the book.
Cover was illustrated with color pencil.

Book design by Israel Rivera.

For Karen, Trevor and Tyler

When I was six, I climbed up a tree.
I sat and dreamed of what I'd grow up to be.

As I started to climb back down,
a tree limb broke, and I fell to the ground.

Police officer Garcia, who had been nearby,
came over and wiped a tear from my eye.

As he bent down to bandage my knee,
he told me to be careful when I climb a tree.

I got on my bike and peddled away.
I rode to the park where I stopped to play.

And then I decided to take a short hike
when I forgot where I'd left my bike.

I turned and started to smile real wide
for police officer Roper had my bike by his side.

Back on my bike, away I flew
because this day was almost through.

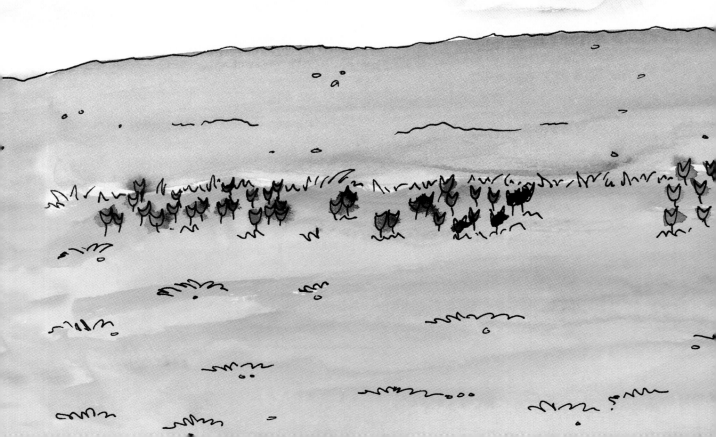

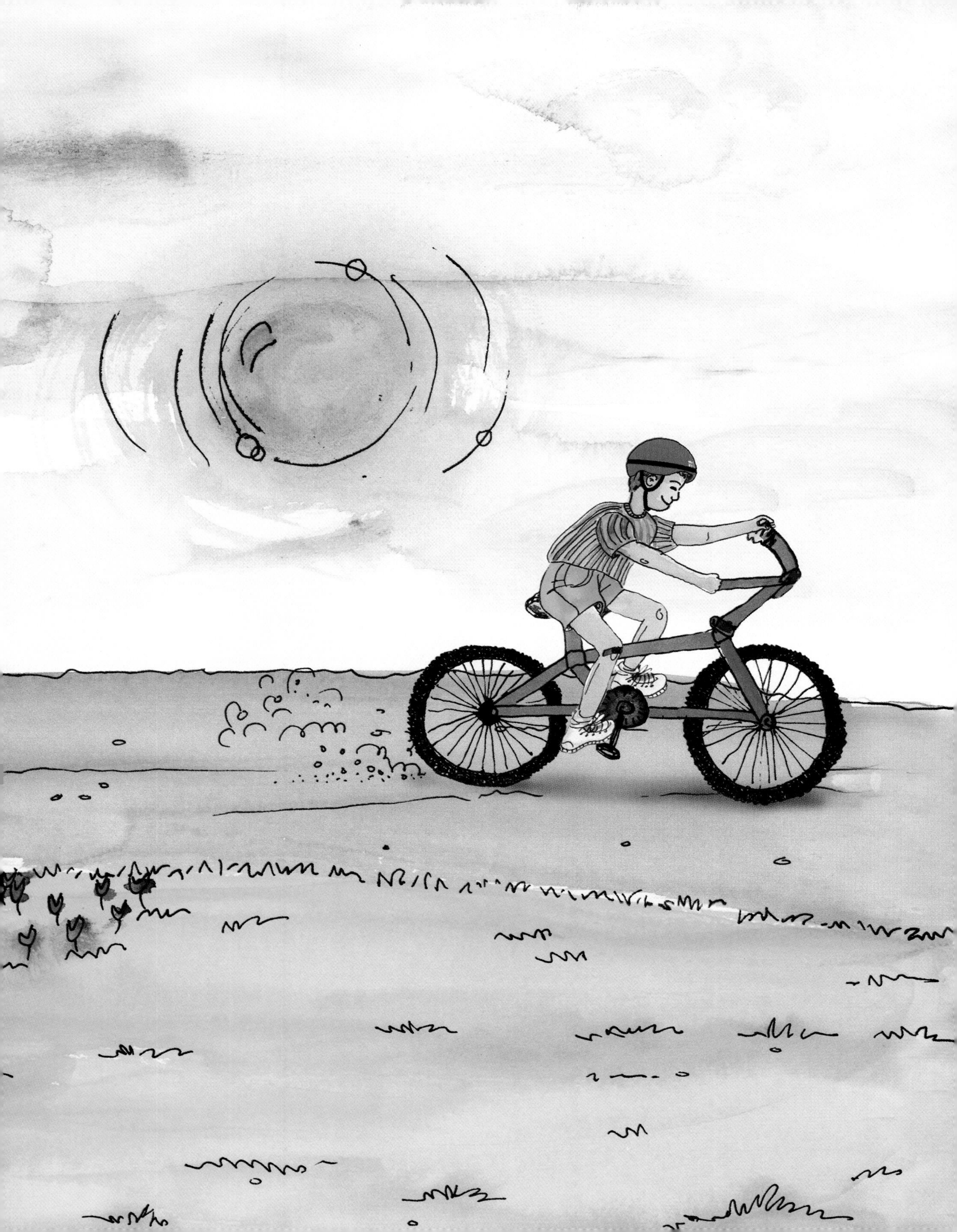

I rode to the street which was busy that day
and found cars going every which way.

Then in a blink, police officer Smith appeared, and he stopped the traffic before it neared.

As I crossed the street, I turned to say
I think I might have lost my way.

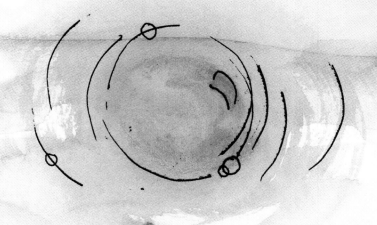

So, police officer Smith put me in his car and said my home was not very far.

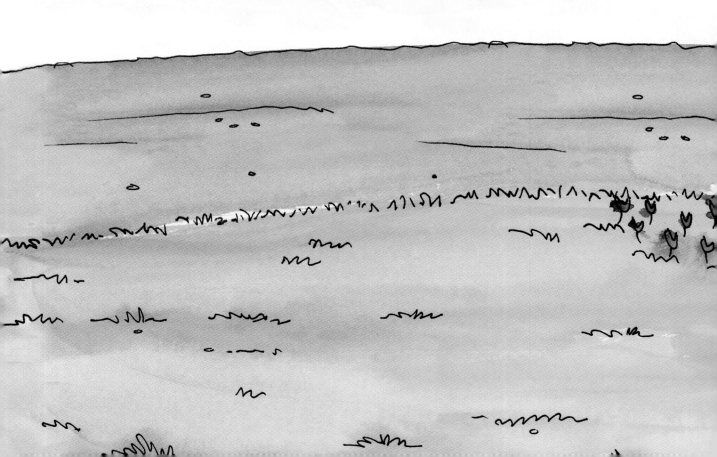

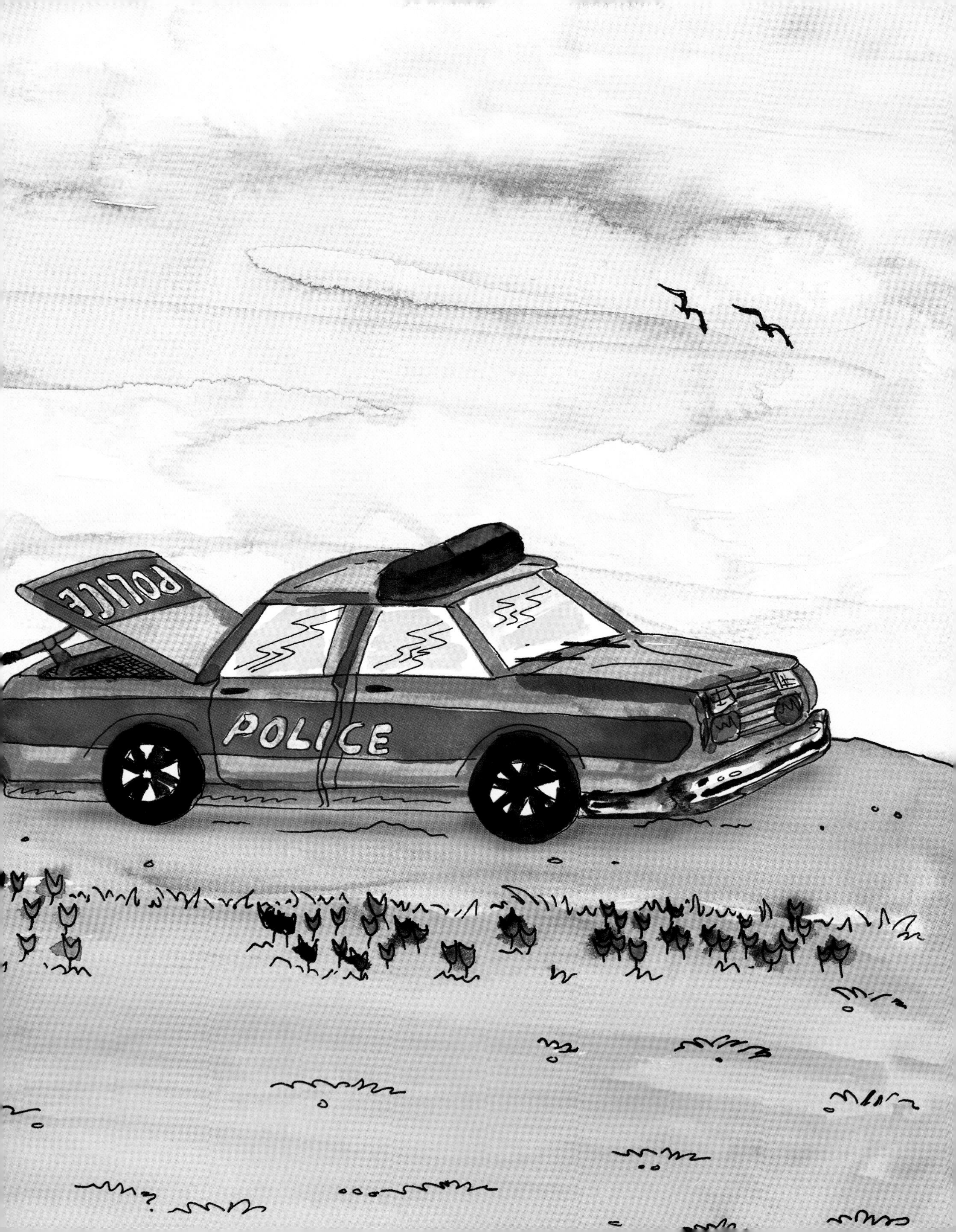
POLICE

He took me home to my mom and dad,
and he told them I was a good, little lad.

As I was lying in my bed that night,
I sat up with all my might.

I said to myself, I know what I'll be...
a police officer like the ones who helped me.

Dallas Senior Corporal Ronald Pinkston wrote this story for his two sons so that they would have a better understanding of how a police officer could help them if they ever needed assistance. It is a story of a little boy who continues to need help after he climbs up a tree and wonders what he would be. The boy later realizes what he wants to be after being helped throughout the day by police officers Garcia, Roper and Smith.

Officer Pinkston would like to thank all the friends who helped make this book possible and to all the men and women in blue who go above and beyond to make sure our children have a safe place to play and grow.